Sleep Tight Tweet Heart

BY JERRY LOTT
PICTURES BY BRAINYINK

Sleep Tight Tweet-Heart

Published by BigStart Publishing

ISBN: 978-1-7636585-6-1

Designs and pictures were taken from freepik.com/Designed by brgfx under freemium license, vecteezy.com under freemium license, Creativefabrica.com under premium license, and Canva.com under premium licencee.

This Book
is dedicated
To all
Awesome
Kids

ZZzzz...

The night has come, and the moon is here
And sleepy heads are heading to dreamland from far and near

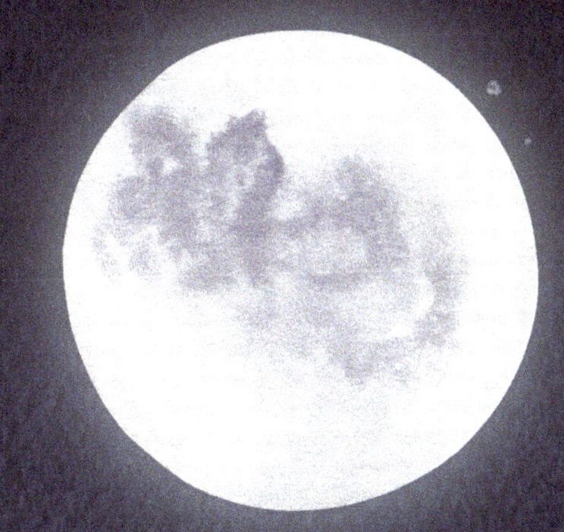

So much love fills the air
before they sleep
All of them wish nighty
night, let's listen and peep

Sleep tight my TWEET- HEART
in your cosy nest

May you have the TWEET-est
sleep and the sweetest rest

May you have a PUURRFECT night my PAW-SOME kitty

Day and night, you're always sweet and always pretty

ZZZ

Good night honey bunny!
With **HOPPY** thoughts of you
I'll sleep

In dreamland too, we'll
play and hop and leap

OWL day, OWL your dreams
will be nice and sweet

Sleep tight my precious,
and shine bright on repeat

A **BEARY** sweet night, in dreamland, you'll have my sweet little bear

Night night baby. Soon I'll see you there

We'll always **BEE**-long
together, even in dreamland

HIVE the sweetest dreams
hon, tomorrow shall be
sweet and grand

Oh sweetheart, my dear
PUP of tea

Goodnight my precious,
PAW-some and sweet
you'll always be

Goodnight sweetheart, let's
SEAL it with a hug and
SEAL it with a kiss

Sweet dreams my dear,
may they be filled with
beauty and bliss

May you have the **SQUEAK**-est dreams and the sweetest night

Goodnight with kisses and a hug so tight

Sweet and warm **FISHES**
to the sweetest fish

You feeling **FIN**-tastic day
and night is all I wish

And to you
my Dear
Sleep
Tight
Sweet
Heart

www.ingramcontent.com/pod-product-compliance
Lightning Source LLC
Chambersburg PA
CBHW042109160726
48295CB00017B/1037

9781763658561